Dear Parent:

Congratulations! Your child is taking the first steps on an exciting journey. The destination? Independent reading!

STEP INTO READING® will help your child get there. The program offers five steps to reading success. Each step includes fun stories and colorful art. There are also Step into Reading Sticker Books, Step into Reading Math Readers, Step into Reading Phonics Readers, Step into Reading Write-In Readers, and Step into Reading Phonics Boxed Sets—a complete literacy program with something to interest every child.

Learning to Read, Step by Step!

Ready to Read   Preschool–Kindergarten
• big type and easy words • rhyme and rhythm • picture clues
For children who know the alphabet and are eager to begin reading.

Reading with Help   Preschool–Grade 1
• basic vocabulary • short sentences • simple stories
For children who recognize familiar words and sound out new words with help.

Reading on Your Own   Grades 1–3
• engaging characters • easy-to-follow plots • popular topics
For children who are ready to read on their own.

Reading Paragraphs   Grades 2–3
• challenging vocabulary • short paragraphs • exciting stories
For newly independent readers who read simple sentences with confidence.

Ready for Chapters   Grades 2–4
• chapters • longer paragraphs • full-color art
For children who want to take the plunge into chapter books but still like colorful pictures.

STEP INTO READING® is designed to give every child a successful reading experience. The grade levels are only guides. Children can progress through the steps at their own speed, developing confidence in their reading, no matter what their grade.

Remember, a lifetime love of reading starts with a single step!

To Mike and Jon, my brave bears and good sons
—S.A.

DISNEY · PIXAR

BRAVE

BIG BEAR, LITTLE BEAR

By Susan Amerikaner

Illustrated by the Disney Storybook Artists

Random House 🏠 New York

Merida climbs SLOWLY.

Angus goes FAST!

The queen is QUIET.

Merida is LOUD.

Fergus and the boys PLAY.

Merida WORKS.

It is DAY.

It is NIGHT.

This man is STRONG.

This man is WEAK.

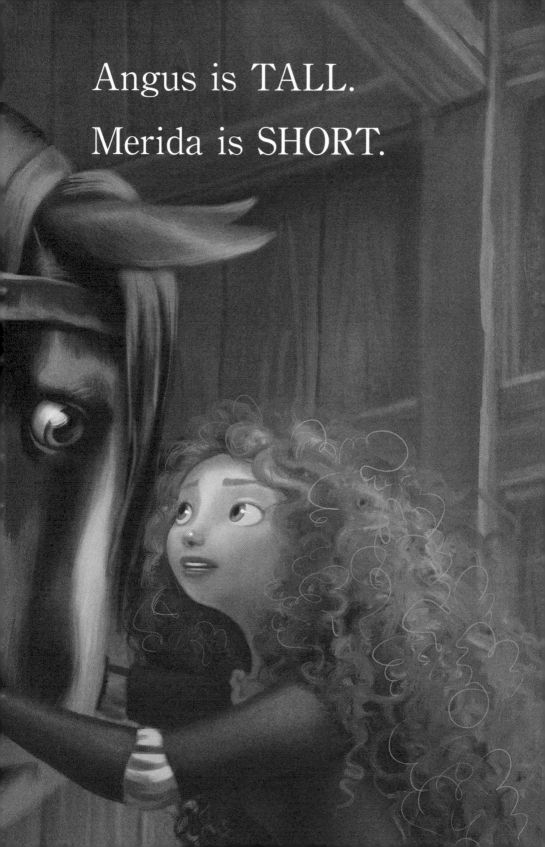

Angus is TALL.

Merida is SHORT.

Merida is NEAR.

Merida is FAR.

The Witch is OLD.

Merida is YOUNG.

The bear stands UP.
Merida falls DOWN.

The bear is DRY.

Merida is WET.

This bear is NICE.

This bear is MEAN.

This bear is BIG.

These bears are SMALL.

Fergus is

IN FRONT OF

Merida.

The bear is

BEHIND Merida.

The triplets are SAD.

The triplets are HAPPY.

Maudie is SCARED.

Merida is BRAVE!